W9-AOT-752

Dear Parent:

Congratulations! Your child is taking the first steps on an exciting journey. The destination? Independent reading!

STEP INTO READING® will help your child get there. The program offers books at five levels that accompany children from their first attempts at reading to reading success. Each step includes fun stories, fiction and nonfiction, and colorful art. There are also Step into Reading Sticker Books, Step into Reading Math Readers, and Step into Reading Phonics Readers— a complete literacy program with something to interest every child.

Learning to Read, Step by Step!

Ready to Read   Preschool–Kindergarten
• big type and easy words • rhyme and rhythm • picture clues
For children who know the alphabet and are eager to begin reading.

Reading with Help   Preschool–Grade 1
• basic vocabulary • short sentences • simple stories
For children who recognize familiar words and sound out new words with help.

Reading on Your Own   Grades 1–3
• engaging characters • easy-to-follow plots • popular topics
For children who are ready to read on their own.

Reading Paragraphs   Grades 2–3
• challenging vocabulary • short paragraphs • exciting stories
For newly independent readers who read simple sentences with confidence.

Ready for Chapters   Grades 2–4
• chapters • longer paragraphs • full-color art
For children who want to take the plunge into chapter books but still like colorful pictures.

STEP INTO READING® is designed to give every child a successful reading experience. The grade levels are only guides. Children can progress through the steps at their own speed, developing confidence in their reading, no matter what their grade.

Remember, a lifetime love of reading starts with a single step!

For my beloved Nanny
—M.L.

Visit us on the Web!
www.stepintoreading.com
www.randomhouse.com/kids
Educators and librarians, for a variety of teaching tools, visit us at
www.randomhouse.com/teachers

Library of Congress Cataloging-in-Publication Data

Lagonegro, Melissa.
Big friend, little friend / by Melissa Lagonegro.
p. cm. — (Step into reading. Step 1 book)
"Disney."
"Princess and Frog."
ISBN 978-0-7364-2644-2 (trade) — ISBN 978-0-7364-8076-5 (lib. bdg.)
I. Princess and the frog (Motion picture) II. Title.
PZ8.L1362Big 2010
[E]—dc22 2009014525

Printed in the United States of America   10 9 8 7 6

DISNEY PRINCESS

THE PRINCESS AND THE FROG

Big Friend,
Little Friend

By Melissa Lagonegro

Illustrated by Elizabeth Tate,
Caroline LaVelle Egan,
Studio IBOIX, Michael Inman,
and the Disney Storybook Artists

Random House 🏠 New York

Tiana and Naveen
are frogs.

The frogs fly

above the crowd.

The alligators are **below** Tiana and Naveen.

It is **daytime**.

It is **nighttime**.

Naveen is **little**.

Louis is **big**.

The frog catchers

stand **up**.

The frog catchers
fall **down**.

Mama Odie is **old**.

Tiana and Naveen

are **young**.

Lawrence is **short**.

Dr. Facilier is **tall**.

Tiana is **first**.

Dr. Facilier is **last**.

Louis swims

under the fireflies.

The stars twinkle
over the friends.

Naveen is **sad**.

Tiana and Naveen
are **happy!**